Tomten Saves Christmas

By Linda Liebrand

Do you remember what you did two days before Christmas Eve last year, really early, at about half past four in the morning? You were probably snoring under your duvet, dreaming about all the lovely Christmas presents you wished for. But Tomten was already up, eating his porridge on the roof of his farm, just like any other day.

You must be wondering who this early riser is, because he almost, but not quite, looks like Santa, doesn't he? Don't be fooled by his long grey beard and short legs though. Tomten might look ancient, and he's only five apples tall, but he is as strong as an ox, and he loves to help the farmer look after the farm and all the animals who live there. But I had probably better tell you that he's quite grumpy and shy around people too, because you'll notice that soon enough anyway. Not even the farmer himself has met him, even though they live on the same farm.

On this very day, two days before Christmas, Tomten was grumpier than usual. He'd been invited for Christmas coffee by his cousin, and namesake, in Norrland, but he really didn't feel like leaving home. 'I like it here at the farm,' he said to Elvira the cat, and scratched her on the chin. 'I don't need to go away to enjoy myself.' The cat rubbed against him and purred, as if she agreed.

Tomten slurped his cup of coffee on his way into the barn, and suddenly he heard his cousin's reindeer landing on the roof. 'How typical. I was just about to go milk the cows, and here comes that braggart of a cousin with the same name as me. Now I have to listen to him boasting about flying reindeer, the Christmas workshop and all the lovely children. Not to mention that annoying Christmas Eve itself — who cares?' Elvira meowed and nodded. 'That boasting show-off hasn't done an honest day's work in his life,' muttered Tomten to the cat, and he hoped his cousin wouldn't be able to find him inside the barn.

Tomten sat down to milk Rosa the cow. It wasn't long before he heard a burst of booming laughter behind his back. 'So this is where you're at!' He recognised his cousin's cheerful voice.

'Hello …' muttered Tomten under his beard. He stood up and was instantly enveloped in a big hug.

'How lovely to see you again, Tomten,' said his cousin, and he laughed again. 'By the way, isn't it funny how we're both called Tomten?' His cousin giggled and held his arms around his big round belly.

'I'm not so sure it's funny exactly,' said Tomten, and he frowned. 'People confuse us all the time and send their wish lists to me every day. My wheelbarrow is full. Look!' Tomten pointed at the wheelbarrow, which was chock-full of letters from all around the world. Just then, his cousin's reindeer came plodding over and started nibbling on the cow's hay and managed to push the barrow with all the letters over.

'No worries, pal. I'll take care of that!' his cousin said as he shuffled the letters into a big sack. 'Let's jump in the sleigh and go to Lappland. I put the coffee on before I left, so it should be done when we get there.'

Tomten reluctantly climbed into the sleigh. While he pulled up a blanket and carefully tucked it in around his legs, Elvira the cat sneaked inside and lay down on a sheepskin on the back seat. Tomten had never been to Norrland, or Lappland. He'd actually never been away from the farm at all, and he held on tight to his hat as they flew high above the forests of Småland. His cousin pointed at something, and Tomten carefully peeked over the edge. 'Can you see the lights down there?' asked his cousin. 'Those are the villages waking up, and they're full of nice kids who've wished for Christmas presents.'

Tomten had never seen the world from this high up. His cousin pointed at lots of landmarks, and Tomten just stared with his jaw dropped. He had no idea the world was this big! Soon they saw the mountains peek up above the horizon, and the reindeer put on the brakes. The landing was bumpy, so Tomten held on tight until the sleigh glided smoothly across the snow. They had landed just in front of a big sign that read 'Workshop — Open'.

Tomten shivered and rubbed his arms to warm up. His breath came out looking like the smoke from a chimney. 'It's really cold here up north, isn't it?' he said to his cousin, who simply jumped out of the sleigh, laughing. But his cousin's workshop and farm looked both warm and inviting, with Advent candles in all the windows, and a huge Christmas tree out in the courtyard. The roofs were covered in thick snow and glimmered so magically in the morning light that Tomten couldn't help but smile. Perhaps a holiday wasn't such a bad idea after all. Elvira jumped out from her hiding place, landed on Tomten's lap and purred happily. 'So you came along too, did you?' chuckled Tomten, and he hugged the cat.

His cousin's helpers ran around the courtyard, with their arms full of strangely wrapped presents of all shapes and sizes. Tomten and Elvira jumped out of the sleigh, and Tomten sighed with relief when he felt the snow creaking under his clogs. His cousin's wife came out and waved hello. The little kids ran around playing happily and pulled Tomten's trouser legs. 'Right, then,' said his cousin. 'Perhaps we could start at the workshop. What do you say?'

'Okay,' said Tomten. 'That sounds good.' They stepped into the workshop, where preparations for Christmas were steaming ahead. Tomten started thinking. 'Well, Christmas Eve is just a few days away, so of course they are busy now. Perhaps I was wrong about my cousin after all. He actually seems to be working really hard here at the workshop!' He could see thousands of Christmas presents stacked floor to ceiling. His cousin's helpers were painting and wrapping balls and trains and dolls and games and other toys that kids had wished for. The tiny helpers were huffing and puffing as they loaded their arms full and carried the gifts out through the door. Tomten thought it looked so heavy that he rolled up his sleeves to help out. 'Hang on,' he called out. 'Just stack them up here, and I'll take care of it all.' He held out his arms, and his cousin's helpers stacked up so many presents that they nearly hit the ceiling.

'Where do these go?' Tomten asked his cousin.

'Ho ho ho, we'll put them out in the stable,' his cousin laughed.

Tomten pulled his brows together and pursed his lips tightly. That didn't sound good, he thought. The stable was the animals' home, not a storage place for gifts. Elvira twitched her tail and followed them into the stable. The aisle was so full of presents that Tomten and the cat could barely pass through. He unloaded the packages onto a hay bale and turned to his cousin. 'Where do the reindeer live now that the stable is so full of clutter?' he asked.

'Come, I'll show you,' replied his cousin happily.

They walked out to the courtyard, and around the corner was a chicken coop. 'The reindeer have moved in here until Christmas is over,' said his cousin. His cheeks turned bright red when he saw Tomten frowning at the mishmash of animals. The reindeer lay criss-crossed on the nesting shelves, and a couple of misplaced chicks played tag among the hooves and muzzles. A feather landed on Elvira's nose, and she batted it away with her paw and growled.

'And where do the poor hens and rooster live now, then?' asked Tomten tensely.

His cousin squirmed and looked embarrassed. 'They live in the doghouse.'

They went to look at the doghouse, where the hens huddled in the dog basket. The rooster had made a nest in the food bowl, and the little chicks played with an abandoned chew bone. Tomten got so angry his ears turned bright red and started to smoke. 'And where do the dogs live now, if I may ask?' he muttered between clenched teeth.

'They share with the goats,' his cousin whispered shyly, and ran up ahead to show the way. And indeed, there in the goats' stable, the dogs were squashed in under the goats' bellies to fit in.

'No, stop. This is bonkers. You can't go on like this!' Tomten called
out, and he waved his fist in the air. 'I have a proposal. We're both
called Tomten, but we're good at different things. I'm Farm Tomten.
And you, you're Yule Tomten. I have a lot of space for packages
and presents at home, in the hayloft at my farm. Why don't you
come there and start wrapping the gifts that are going south?
You can still use the workshop for the gifts that are going north.
Then I'll call for the moose — they'll love to help pulling the cart. We
can use the old horse cart, and we'll all help delivering the gifts.'

'Oh, you're so kind helping us out,' smiled his relieved cousin. 'Thank you so very much!'

Tomten blushed under his beard. 'Oh, but of course, I'm here for you. What else is family for?' They both laughed and started to load the Christmas presents onto the sleigh. Tomten took the reindeer back into their stable, the hens could go back to their coop, and the dogs curled up in their baskets again. When everyone was back in their right place, Tomten smiled with relief, and the two cousins and the cat flew back south to Tomten's farm.

The hayloft was a perfect place to store presents. They used hay bales to make tables and chairs, and they stacked presents all the way up to the ceiling. On Christmas Eve, they got up early and started loading the presents onto the horse cart. Yule Tomten handed a bag to Farm Tomten. 'Here's a bag of flying powder. Give it to the moose and the horses, along with a handful of oats, and things will go much faster!' Tomten nodded delightedly and thanked him. Then off they went to fly from house to house, knocking on the nice children's doors. If anyone was surprised to have their Christmas presents delivered by the small, grey Farm Tomten instead of Yule Tomten, they didn't say a word about it.

In the evening, when Tomten and all the animals came back home to Yule Tomten's workshop, they were met by a wonderful smell. Christmas ham, meatballs and Jansson's temptation. And of course, Christmas porridge! Mrs Tomten had cooked a wonderful Christmas meal for everyone at the farm. Tomten's belly grumbled, and Elvira meowed happily, spying all the good food. Perhaps leaving home every now and then to see the family wasn't such a bad idea after all, thought Tomten as he spooned up a big bowl full of porridge. Elvira sneaked up onto the table and scoffed a big meatball before anyone had a chance to shoo her away. Tomten found a small roll-shaped present without a tag tied to his spoon. He opened it carefully and rolled out the piece of paper he found inside.

'One return ticket to Lappland' it said, and there was a small bag of flying powder too. 'We hope you come back and see us real soon,' laughed Yule Tomten, and Farm Tomten clapped his hands with glee. The warmth from the porridge spread from his tummy, through his body, and Tomten felt so happy among friends and family.

Yes, that's how Farm Tomten and Yule Tomten became best friends last year. So don't be surprised if your Christmas presents are delivered by a small, grey Tomten this year. But whatever you do, don't forget to put out a bowl of porridge for him, or else he becomes that awful grumpy Tomten again.

Now, perhaps you're wondering who's been telling this story? Go back and look at all the pictures again. Can you see someone who came along on Tomten's trip to Lappland? That's right. Elvira the cat, that's me. And just for the record, I got more than one meatball that Christmas. Miaow!

A note on the Swedish names, foods and places you'll read about in this story

Norrland could be translated as 'the Northlands' and is the northernmost part of Sweden. Lappland is one of the nine historical provinces of Norrland. Småland is a province in southern Sweden.

Yule Tomten, or jultomten in Swedish, is the Swedish Santa Claus, who brings children Christmas presents on Christmas Eve.

Farm Tomten, or gårdstomten in Swedish, is the farm gnome, who helps guard and look after the farm in Swedish folklore.

Christmas porridge tastes very similar to rice pudding, and traditionally, a bowl of porridge is left out for Tomten on Christmas Eve as a way to say thank you.

Christmas ham and meatballs, along with the creamy potato and anchovy dish called Jansson's temptation, are other typically Swedish Christmas foods.

Some things to talk about after you've read this book

- How did the cat and Tomten show their emotions?

- Why do you think Tomten didn't want to leave his farm to begin with?

- How did Tomten's feelings change throughout the story?

- Why do you think Tomten got upset when he saw the reindeer and the animals living in the wrong places?

- What do you think the difference is between Farm Tomten and Yule Tomten?

- What was Tomten's favourite food?

- They had meatballs, Christmas ham and Jansson's temptation to eat on Christmas Eve. What do you eat with your family for Christmas?

Hi. I'm Linda. I'm a Swedish mum living among the rolling green hills of Surrey in the United Kingdom, together with my Dutch husband, bouncy toddler and boisterous Swiss dog. As you can tell, we're an international bunch, and we speak English at home. I grew up in Sweden, reading enchanting stories about Farm Tomten and forest trolls — and now I write children's books about Swedish folklore and traditions to share my cultural heritage with our young bookworm. I hope your little explorers will enjoy the books too, while learning about all things Swedish.

If you've enjoyed this book, please consider leaving an honest review where you bought it, as it will help other parents find and choose it too. I'd love to stay in touch. You can find me on Instagram (@Linda_Liebrand) and Facebook (@SwenglishLife).

Do you believe in Tomten?
Get a Free Tomten poster with gorgeous illustrations from this book. Ask a grown-up to visit www.swenglish.life/tomtenposter to download your free poster

I believe in
Tomten

More books by Linda Liebrand

These are some of my bilingual books about Sweden. They are perfect for kids who're learning both Swedish and English.

Counting Sweden — Räkna med Sverige
One Midsummer pole, two Vikings or three crowns? Just imagine how many typically Swedish things there are to count. Kids will have fun counting from one to ten while learning to recognise some of Sweden's most loved national symbols and traditions.

My first book about Sweden — Min första bok om Sverige
From lingonberries to Falu red cottages and Vikings, this picture book introduces Swedish traditions, culture and everyday fun. Both kids and adults will love the gorgeous colour photos.

The Easter Party — Påskfesten
A fun Easter story for kids aged 3–6. At the end of the book, they'll learn more about Easter eggs, Easter witches, Easter twigs and other typically Swedish Easter traditions.

Santa's Christmas — Tomtens Jul
A counting book that you and your toddler will enjoy reading together. They'll discover some Swedish Christmas words and have lots of fun counting from one to fifteen with Santa.

I'm always writing new books, so be sure to check my website for the latest news. www.swenglish.life

Made in the USA
Las Vegas, NV
13 December 2022

62338603R00021